Nationals
Park

Washington
Metro

Smithsonian
Castle

National Archives

ON THE LOOSE
IN WASHINGTON, D.C

Dear Animal Detectives,

The animals included in this book are ones I thought you would recognize and have fun finding (at least in these pages) on the streets of Washington. Many of them can be found at the National Zoo. Because the zoo is constantly moving animals to other zoos around the country and bringing in new animals from countries around the globe, it's always exciting to find out what animals the zoo has at any given time. For a look at the 2,000 animals from 400 species that currently live at the zoo, you can visit the National Zoo online at http://nationalzoo.si.edu. Or, better yet, visit the zoo in person. As with all other Smithsonian Institution exhibits and museums in D.C., admission is free.

Sy. Shd

P.S. In real life the zoo does an excellent job making sure its animals are very happy at home, and don't go wandering off!...

ON THE LOOSE
IN WASHINGTON, D.C.

A Find-the-Animals Book

Written and Illustrated
by Sage Stossel

Commonwealth Editions
Carlisle, Massachusetts

ISBN 978-1-938700-14-9

Commonwealth Editions is an imprint of Applewood Books Inc.,
Carlisle, Massachusetts 01741.
Visit us on the web at www.commonwealtheditions.com.

Visit Sage Stossel on the web at www.sagestossel.com.

Printed in the U.S.A.

10 9 8 7 6 5 4 3 2

In the capital city
of this mighty land
lies our National Zoo
with an aspect quite grand.

One morning the keeper
discovered a note.
"We've gone for a walk,"
the animals wrote.

"Oh, dear," said the keeper,
"what am I to do?
My critters have left me
alone at the zoo!"

The cages, indeed, were all empty that day,
for the creatures, it seemed, had meandered away.

2 pandas, 1 hippo, 1 tiger, 2 lemurs, 1 alligator, 1 koala bear, 1 turtle, 1 elephant, 3 monkeys, 1 ostrich, 1 polar bear, 1 antelope, 2 kangaroos, 1 penguin, 1 parrot, 1 groundhog, 3 snakes, 1 donkey, 1 frog, 1 lion, and 2 giraffes? (Do you also see 4 cat statues and a bear statue on the zoo roof?)

CAN YOU FIND

Then the president called with an urgent report:
"There are pigs on my lawn and they're starting to snort!"

4 pigs, 1 lion, 1 penguin, 4 giraffes, 1 donkey, 1 elephant, 1 turtle, 2 kangaroos, 1 ostrich, 1 camel, 1 moose, 2 monkeys, 1 antelope, 1 rhinoceros, 1 panda, 2 koala bears, 1 brown bear, 1 snake, and 1 lemur?

CAN YOU FIND

A commotion next broke out on Capitol Hill
when a donkey and elephant hashed out a bill.

1 donkey, 1 elephant, 3 giraffes, 1 penguin, 1 antelope, 1 lion, 1 rhinoceros, 1 panda, 1 kangaroo, 2 monkeys, 1 camel, 1 koala bear, 1 large white bird, 1 snake, and 1 polar bear?

CAN YOU FIND

Our land's highest judges weren't sure what to do
when the court was approached by a large kangaroo.

2 kangaroos, 1 zebra, 1 elephant, 1 giraffe, 1 alligator, 1 snake, 2 antelope, 1 panda,
2 rhinoceros, 1 ostrich, 2 donkeys, 1 camel, 2 lions, 1 turtle, 2 koala bears,
1 monkey, and 9 Supreme Court justices in black robes?

CAN YOU FIND

A complaint was next lodged via telephone call:
"There's a lion at large on the National Mall!"

1 lion, 1 giraffe, 2 kangaroos, 1 alligator, 1 ostrich, 1 elephant, 1 penguin, 1 snake, 1 turtle, 1 tiger, 1 donkey, 1 lemur, 1 koala bear, and 1 panda?

CAN YOU FIND

The Library of Congress soon got a bit loud,
until someone explained, "There's no squawking allowed!"

1 snake, 1 rhinoceros, 2 lions, 1 kangaroo, 1 panda, 1 red-and-white bird, 1 zebra, 3 ostriches, 1 brown bear, 1 turtle, 2 penguins, 1 moose, 1 antelope, 2 monkeys, 1 elephant, 1 lemur, and 1 koala bear?

CAN YOU FIND

Next the Lincoln Memorial suffered a scare
when a rattlesnake slithered right up the front stairs.

3 snakes, 2 turtles, 1 lemur, 1 brown bear, 1 koala, 1 rhinoceros, 1 penguin, 1 antelope, 1 hippo, 1 alligator, 1 ostrich, 2 kangaroos, 2 monkeys, 1 donkey, 1 elephant, 4 giraffes, 1 panda, 1 lion, and 1 camel?

CAN YOU FIND

At the big Tidal Basin, boat rentals went fine
'til an ornery ostrich cut into the line.

1 ostrich, 2 hippos, 1 tiger, 1 penguin, 3 snakes, 1 lion, 2 elephants, 1 koala bear, 2 giraffes, 3 monkeys, 2 alligators, 2 kangaroos, 1 brown bear, and 1 rhinoceros?

CAN YOU FIND

At the Air and Space Museum the staff was impressed
by the wide range of species who showed up as guests.

2 alligators, 1 giraffe, 2 snakes, 2 koala bears, 1 lion, 1 panda, 1 elephant, 2 kangaroos, 1 rhinoceros, 2 lemurs, 1 turtle, 2 monkeys, and 1 brown bear?

CAN YOU FIND

Meanwhile, hip Dupont Circle was quite the wild scene
with an antelope walking around on the green.

1 antelope, 1 rhinoceros, 1 giraffe, 2 monkeys, 1 brown bear, 2 lemurs, 1 owl, 2 snakes,
1 kangaroo, 1 koala bear, 1 groundhog, 1 elephant, 1 penguin, 1 turtle, 1 tiger, and 1 alligator?

CAN YOU FIND

Even picturesque Georgetown was roused by a roar
when a trio of tigers sang songs by a store.

3 tigers, 1 elephant, 1 koala bear, 2 giraffes, 2 penguins, 1 groundhog, 1 brown bear, 1 lion,
1 kangaroo, 3 snakes, 1 rhinoceros, 1 camel, 1 antelope, 2 monkeys, 1 lemur, 1 ostrich, and 1 turtle?

CAN
YOU
FIND

When at last night descended
the zookeeper smiled,
as back through the gate
all his animals filed.

What a wonderful day
they appeared to have had,
but to be back at home
they seemed equally glad.

As for where they had been
they refused to confess,
but the keeper was smart
and could probably guess.

CAN YOU HELP
THESE ANIMALS
FIND THEIR WAY
HOME TO THE
ZOO?

SAGE STOSSEL is a contributing editor for the *Atlantic* and a cartoonist for the *Boston Globe*, theatlantic.com, the *Provincetown Banner* (for which she received a New England Press Association Award), and elsewhere. Her cartoons have been featured by the *New York Times Week in Review*, CNN *Headline News*, Best Editorial Cartoons of the Year, and other venues. Her children's book *On the Loose in Boston* was published by Commonwealth Editions (an imprint of Applewood Books) in 2009. She is currently at work on a graphic novel, *Starling*, forthcoming from Penguin.

More Online...

Visit onthelooseindc.com for Washington pictures to print and color, fun facts about the city, puzzles and mazes, ideas for things to do around D.C., and more.

Kramerbooks
& Afterwords
Cafe

Marine Corps
Iwo Jima Memorial

Eisenhower
Executive
Office Building